This book is dedicated to my dad,

Bob Morgan, and to all the Papas of the world who fiercely love their grandchildren, family, and magical holiday traditions. In your last moments on earth, you asked me to finish this for you and I hope you are proud. Dad, we love you now and forever.

www.mascotbooks.com

For more information, please contact:
Mascot Books
620 Herndon Parkway, Suite 320
Herndon, VA 20170
info@mascotbooks.com

Library of Congress Control Number: 2018907800

CPSIA Code: PRT0918A
ISBN-13: 978-1-68401-707-2

Printed in the United States

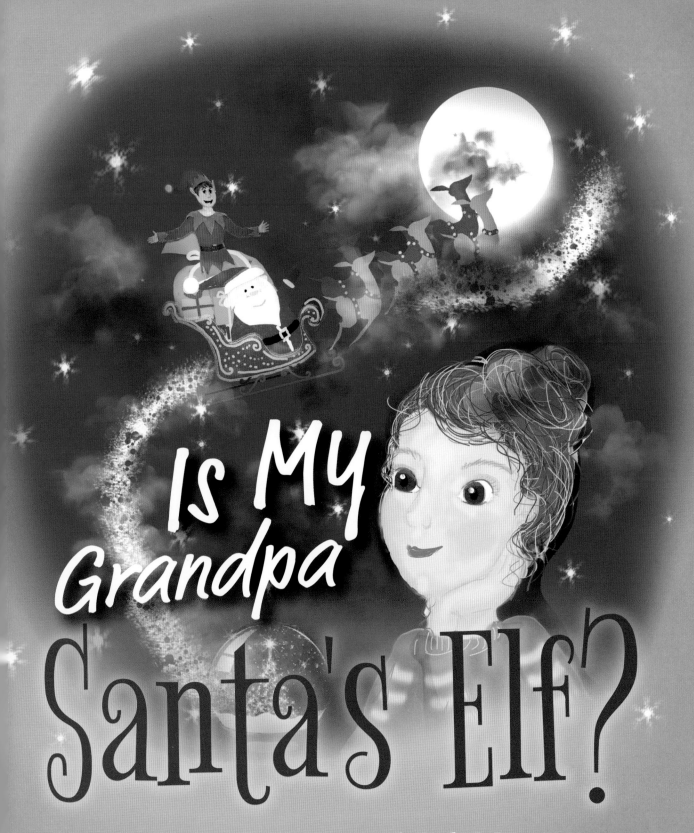

Is My Grandpa
Santa's Elf?

Heather Zivkovich and Bob Morgan

Illustrated by Monica Nicolosi

Kay Rose

Hi, my name is Kay Rose! I am eight years old, and my most favorite day of the whole year is Christmas. I am the oldest of eight grandkids, and everyone—and I mean EVERYONE—always says we inherited our Christmas heart from our Grandpa Bob.

What the heck is a Christmas heart, you might say? Was my Grandpa Bob born with a sparkly red and green heart? Maybe it even lights up like a Christmas light? Well, yes and no...

Grandpa Bob has always seemed extra magical. Every day, he wakes up and puts on his Christmas sweater. Then he drinks his special hot cocoa while singing Christmas carols on his way out to walk his dog Vixen. Yep, you heard me right! His dog's name is Vixen. Do you want to know what Vixen's favorite thing to do is? Play in the snow!

My grandma has to hide all the cookies in the house, or else Grandpa Bob will eat them all. He even insists on leaving the Christmas decorations up all year long.

Between you and me, I think my grandpa is an elf! Being the oldest of eight grandkids, it's my job to figure this out. But I have to keep this a secret from the rest of them until I find out the truth. I don't want to get their hopes up just yet...

Christmas Eve is only a few days away, so here's my plan. I overheard
Grandpa Bob talking about an old Christmas photo album hidden
somewhere in his house. I only heard bits and pieces, but it sounded
like a really magical story. So if I can find that, then all my questions
will be answered! Luckily, today all the grandkids are headed over
to his house to make Christmas cookies, help decorate the tree, and
have a sleepover. All I have to do is slip away from the holly jolly
festivities and find his old magical Christmas photo album.

So scratch that! Things did not go as planned. Grandpa Bob kept such a close eye on me that I wasn't able to sneak away.

Now it's late and I am trying to stay awake while snuggled in my sleeping bag.

Just then, I spotted some super-duper sparkly gold dust in the air that smelled like candy canes. I love candy canes, so I followed it.

It led me to a small door in Grandpa Bob's closet that had old Christmas cards taped over it. And inside—*THERE IT WAS!* The old magical Christmas photo album! But just as I was about to open it, I heard a creak behind me.

Kay Rose
Quin
Wynter
Grace
AJ
Isaac
Edison
Annie
Everett
Carly
Erin
Bob
K.

It was Grandpa Bob! I had been caught and probably now on the extra-naughty list for snooping around. But instead, he asked how I had found the hiding place of his secret old magical Christmas album.

I told him about the candy-cane-scented super sparkly gold dust in the air, and I also confessed that I thought for sure he was one of Santa's elves.

By then, the sun was starting to come up. Grandpa
Bob told me to get ready, because I was joining him
with hot cocoa in hand on his morning walk with
Vixen. *I'm going to be in so much trouble with Santa*, I
kept thinking over and over again. Out the door
we went while everyone else was still dreaming of
sugary sweet plums.

As we walked, it began to snow. Not just any kind of snow—it was the super-duper extra sparkly magical kind of snow. It felt like it was just me and Grandpa Bob in our very own snowglobe. He told me he knew this day would eventually come, so I put my hand out, expecting to get my very first lump of coal.

But to my surprise, Grandpa Bob put his magical photo album in my hands and invited me to look through it. At that moment, all my questions were finally answered. Grandpa Bob was indeed an elf!

He wasn't one of the elves who made Christmas presents for all the kids in the world, or one of the elves who kept track of the naughty or nice list. You see, he was one of the highest and most powerful of Santa's elves.

Years ago, when Grandpa Bob was six, he woke up in the middle of the night on Christmas Eve and met Santa. After seeing how much Grandpa Bob loved Christmas, Santa decided to give him the most magical gift that ever existed—his Christmas heart!

From then on, he was Santa's main heart of the world, or *"Spirit Elf"* as Santa called it in the official document.

My Grandpa Bob was the head Christmas Spirit Elf of the world, and his job was to spread the love, joy, kindness, and giving of the Christmas season all year long.

So there you have it! Grandpa Bob is one of Santa's main men!

So now that I have my answer, I can finally go and tell my cousins, right? Wrong. Grandpa Bob made me promise to keep his secret until the rest of the cousins are old enough to learn about his magical secret on their own.

In return, he gave me some of my very own super-duper sparkly gold dust in a small heart glass jar.

I will never forget the pictures I saw in Grandpa Bob's magical photo album on that snowy morning. He was given the best gift EVER—a heart overflowing in endless Christmas love, and the job to be Santa's Spirit Elf.

I can't wait to talk about this with the rest of the cousins, but for now I will look at my magical super-duper sparkly gold dust and live every day with the joy, love, and spirit of Christmas in my heart.

Oh, I almost forgot. Will you *PLEASE,* with sugarplums on top, keep our Christmas secret, too? It would mean the world to Grandpa Bob, and who knows? Maybe a bit of his Christmas spirit will find its way into your heart!

Close your eyes.

Do you smell candy canes? Well you should, because I just threw some of my sparkly gold dust into your heart. We can call that our Christmas gift to you. Merry Christmas, and like Grandpa Bob always says, keep the traditions alive forever.

About the Author

Heather Zivkovich and her dad, Bob Morgan, partner up in *Is My Grandpa Santa's Elf?* to deliver Christmas magic and spirit to the hearts of the world. Bob Morgan stands for the fierce love of his family, holidays, and traditions. He wants the world to live in peace and find the joy in living every day like it's Christmas.